The Kingdom of Wrenly

6

Beneath the Stone Forest

By Jordan Quinn
Illustrated by Robert McPhillips

LITTLE SIMON

New York   London   Toronto   Sydney   New Delhi

LITTLE SIMON
An imprint of Simon & Schuster Children's Publishing Division
1230 Avenue of the Americas, New York, New York 10020
First Little Simon paperback edition December 2014
Copyright © 2014 by Simon & Schuster, Inc.
Also available in a Little Simon hardcover edition.
All rights reserved, including the right of reproduction in whole or in part in any form.
LITTLE SIMON is a registered trademark of Simon & Schuster, Inc., and associated colophon is a trademark of Simon & Schuster, Inc.
For information about special discounts for bulk purchases, please contact
Simon & Schuster Special Sales at 1-866-506-1949 or business@simonandschuster.com.
The Simon & Schuster Speakers Bureau can bring authors to your live event. For more information or to book an event contact the Simon & Schuster Speakers Bureau at 1-866-248-3049 or visit our website at www.simonspeakers.com.
Manufactured in the United States of America 0417 MTN
6 8 10 9 7 5
Library of Congress Cataloging-in-Publication Data
Quinn, Jordan.
Beneath the Stone Forest / by Jordan Quinn ; illustrated by Robert McPhillips.
pages cm. — (The Kingdom of Wrenly ; 6)
Summary: Clara invites Prince Lucas on her journey to map out the Stone Forest and visit the gnomes who live there.
ISBN 978-1-4814-1391-6 (paperback) — ISBN 978-1-4814-1392-3 (hc)
ISBN 978-1-4814-1393-0 (ebook)
[1. Princes—Fiction. 2. Adventure and adventurers—Fiction.]
I. McPhillips, Robert, illustrator. II. Title.
PZ7.Q31945Be 2014 [Fic]—dc23
2014005189

CONTENTS

CHAPTER 1

Daydreamer

Mistress Carson pointed to a map of the Kingdom of Wrenly. The map was worn around the edges and had begun to fade.

"Clara, please name the tallest peak in Flatfrost," she said, looking directly at her star pupil.

The classroom was quiet.

"Clara?" repeated her teacher.

But Clara didn't answer. She

hadn't heard a word her teacher had said. She sat and gazed out the window, daydreaming. Her boots scuffed back and forth underneath

her bench. Clara loved geography, and whenever the subject came up in school she would daydream about her next adventure with her best friend, Prince Lucas.

Madeline, the girl who sat beside Clara, nudged her elbow.

"Umph!" groaned Clara as she sat up straight.

Her classmates laughed. Clara's face flushed. *Oh no!* she thought. *I've been caught daydreaming! How embarrassing!* Clara looked at her

teacher. Mistress Carson repeated the question.

"The tallest peak in Flatfrost is Mount Linton," said Clara. She had just been to Flatfrost with Lucas, so she knew exactly where it was.

"Thank you, Clara," said Mistress Carson. "Class, today I have a special

geography assignment. I want everyone to research a place in the kingdom they haven't been to. Talk to the
people who live there, and observe
their land. Find out as many details
as you can. Then write about the
place and draw a map and picture
of what it looks like on a piece of
animal hide, which I'll pass out. I'll
also hand out charcoal for you to
draw your scenes. You will present
your projects a week from
today."

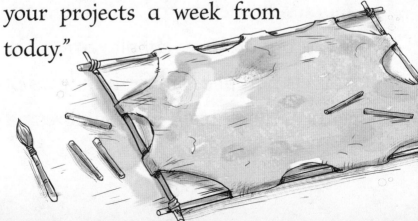

Some of the children moaned at the thought of a new assignment. Others began to talk excitedly about where they might go. Clara had always wanted to explore the Stone Forest.

The Stone Forest, in the south of Wrenly's mainland, was a grove of stone pillars and arches, formed by gnomes tunneling for gems beneath the ground. The rubble from the tunnels had piled up for hundreds of years and created a fanciful forest of

stone towers, steeples, and arches.

Clara had heard about the maze of gemstone tunnels that lay beneath the Stone Forest. She had also heard that the gnomes were the only ones who had ever been able to mine the gems. For everyone else, the gems

were permanently stuck to the cavern walls.

I can't wait to tell Lucas, thought Clara. *This assignment will be the perfect chance for us to explore a new place.*

The best part was that they'd be able to go today: Mistress Carson let school out before lunch!

CHAPTER 2

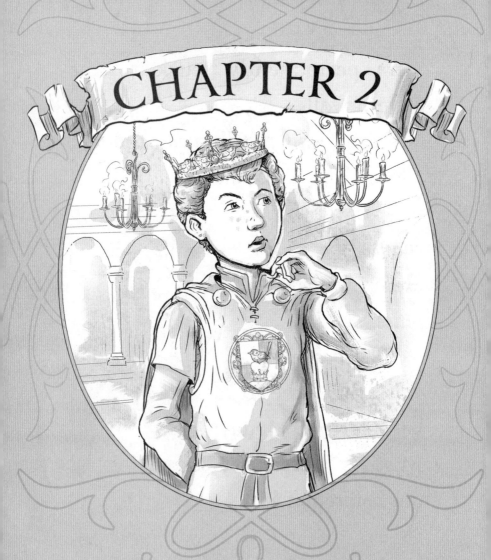

Bella and Percy

Lucas pulled at the collar around his neck. His mother had asked him to dress in his finest clothes. His uncle and aunt, King Rufus and Queen Eleanor of Kestrel, were due to arrive at the castle shortly with their daughter, Princess Arabella (or Bella, as everyone called her).

Lucas sighed loudly. He could hardly move in his starched linen undergarments and blue silk jacket. His jacket had the family crest embroidered on the front. Lucas

looked at himself in the mirror. He had to admit, the crest made him feel important, but the rest of the outfit made him feel like a prisoner trapped in his own clothes.

"Mother, I can't breathe," he complained.

"You'll get used to it," said Queen Tasha. "You have to wear your good clothes for Cousin Bella. Remember, she'll be dressed like a proper royal too."

"Ugh," Lucas murmured.

"And please try not to ruin your good clothes this afternoon," added his mother.

Lucas nodded, even though he knew that there was a good chance of that happening.

Then the royal trumpets sounded and the drummers began to drum.

Lucas's family hurried to the great hall and stood side by side to greet their guests. Lucas heard a shrill bark.

Yap! Yap! Yap! went the sound. *Yip! Yap! Yip!*

Ruskin, Lucas's pet red dragon, cocked his head and began to growl. Smoke trickled from his nostrils.

"Easy, Ruskin," Lucas said firmly. "It's only a dog."

Ruskin settled down at Lucas's command. King Rufus and Queen Eleanor entered the great hall,

followed by Princess Bella. Bella held a small, fluffy white dog in her arms. The dog yapped all the way across the room.

The yaps echoed throughout the

hall. King Caleb put a hand over one of his ears. Queen Tasha raised an eyebrow. Princess Bella made no attempt to quiet her dog. She walked

gracefully across the room with her dainty nose up in the air.

The princess had a long braid

of golden hair and green eyes. A circlet of twisted silk fit snugly on the crown of her head, and a lovely jewel dangled in the middle of her forehead. She wore a long gown of fine purple silk with bell sleeves and matching satin shoes. Bella gave Lucas a cool glance.

Lucas forced a smile.

Yap! Yap! Yip! The princess's fluffy white

dog demanded to be introduced.

"When did you get a dog?" asked Lucas, trying to show interest.

"For my eighth birthday," said Bella. "His name is Percy."

Ruskin squawked playfully at Percy. Percy growled. Ruskin snorted

and looked at Lucas as if to say, *Is it okay to growl now?*

"No," Lucas said to Ruskin.

Ruskin dropped his head and stood by his master.

Bella gave Lucas a disgusted look. "Please keep your serpent at a distance. He's scaring Percy."

"Don't worry," said Lucas. "Ruskin won't hurt your little fur ball."

"I should hope not," she replied.

Lucas sighed. How was he

supposed to pass a whole day with his unpleasant cousin? The grown-ups laughed and talked noisily. They seemed to be having a great time.

"Would you like to go to the play-room?" asked Lucas, trying to sound cheerful.

"I suppose so," said Bella. "Does that overgrown lizard have to come?"

"His name is Ruskin," said Lucas. "And he's a good dragon. And yes, he's going to come with us."

"Hmph," said Bella.

Ruskin squawked and bounded after Lucas. The princess and her dog followed at a safe distance.

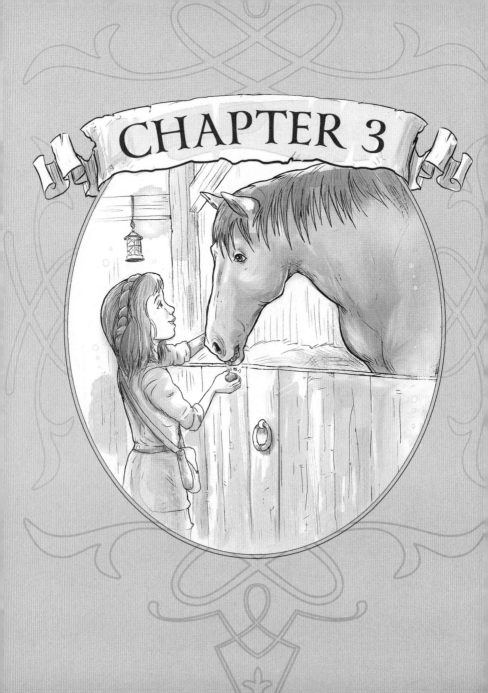

CHAPTER 3

Peasant Girl

Clara ran down the lane and up the hill toward the castle. She had some animal hides for her class geography project tucked in her pocket. *I can't wait to tell Lucas the plan,* she thought.

First, Clara stopped by the royal stables to give her horse, Scallop, a carrot muffin from her father's bakery. A fancy horse and carriage was

parked near the stall. *The palace must have visitors,* she thought.

Clara hugged Scallop and rubbed her cheek along her horse's neck. Then she ran up the back stairs to the palace. She opened the heavy oak door and bumped right into her mother, Anna Gills, Queen Tasha's seamstress.

"Hello, honey," her mother said. "I was just on my way to town to pick up some thread. Lucas is in the playroom with Princess Bella."

"Princess who?" questioned Clara.

"Princess Bella," repeated her mother. "Lucas's cousin. Be sure to curtsy when you meet her, and please stay away from the throne room. The king and queen are entertaining."

I wonder what Princess Bella is like, thought Clara as she watched her mother tap down the stone stairs. *And curtsy?* she wondered. *I've never had to curtsy for Lucas.* But then again, she never thought of Lucas as royalty. She knew he was a prince, but they had been friends for so long, she never had to behave formally around him.

Clara went inside and bounded up the stairs to the playroom. She swung open the door, and it banged against the wall accidentally. Bella's dog growled and scampered toward Clara.

"Be quiet, Percy!" ordered Bella as she looked Clara up and down.

"Lucas, why is there a peasant girl in your playroom?"

Clara's face flushed. *Peasant girl?* she thought. *Well, I suppose I am a peasant girl*. But suddenly it sounded like a disease.

"This is my friend Clara," said Lucas. "My father has allowed her

to visit the castle anytime."

"Is that a joke?" asked Bella, keeping her eyes fixed on Clara.

Ruskin squawked. He didn't like the princess's tone of voice.

"Watch what you

say, Bella," said Lucas. "Clara is my *best* friend."

Bella rolled her eyes and folded her arms. "Fine. Then she should curtsy and kiss my hand like a proper subject."

Clara's mouth dropped open. She felt more like throwing up than

curtsying. But Clara knew she had
to follow the royal rules. She took
a deep breath, walked up to Bella,
and curtsied. Then Bella lifted her

soft, milky white hand up to Clara's face. Clara shut her eyes and quickly kissed the back of the princess's hand. It smelled like dog.

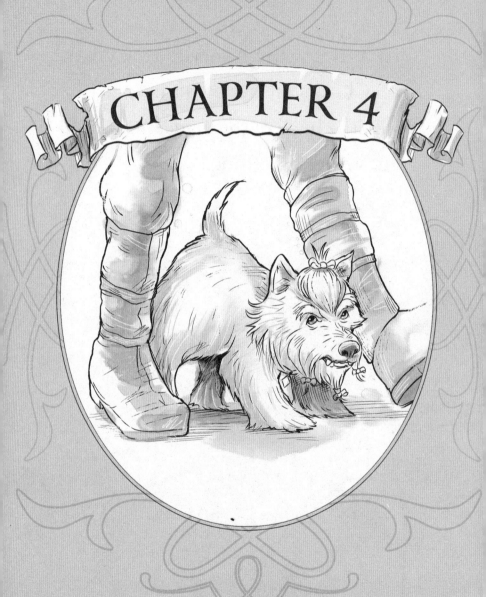

CHAPTER 4

All That Glitters

Percy sniffed Clara's boots. Then Clara took a giant step over Percy and walked toward Lucas.

"So, guess what?" said Clara as she tried to ignore Bella's watchful eye.

"What?" asked Lucas.

"I have an idea for our next adventure."

Lucas's eyes widened. He loved it

when Clara got ideas. "What is it?"

"My teacher said we have to research a place in Wrenly that we haven't been to before," Clara explained.

"Where *haven't* you been?" Lucas asked.

"The Stone Forest," said Clara. "Have you ever been there?"

"I've only seen it from the road," said Lucas.

"Same here," said Clara.

Then Bella huffed. "Why would *anyone* want to go *there*?" she questioned. "Isn't it just a bunch of crummy old towers and creepy dark tunnels?"

Clara almost said, *Who asked you?* But she stopped herself. If Bella didn't want to go to the Stone Forest, then Lucas wouldn't be able to go either. *Hmm,* thought Clara. *How can I make this adventure sound like one that Bella would want to go on?*

She took a good look at the princess. Then she noticed the lovely gemstone hanging in the middle of the princess's forehead. It gave Clara an idea.

"Bella, did you know the most beautiful jewels in the kingdom come from the Stone Forest?" she asked. "Those creepy underground tunnels are just bursting with precious gems."

Bella's eyes lit up. "Precious gems?" she repeated.

"Tons of sparkling jewels *everywhere!*" insisted Clara.

Bella set down her dog and clasped her hands. "I *love* jewelry!"

she exclaimed. "When do we leave?"

"As soon as possible," Clara said.

"Okay, I'll go," said the princess, "but on one condition."

"What?" asked Clara.

"That we take a carriage," said Bella. "I don't want to rumple my dress sitting on top of a horse."

"It's a deal!" said Lucas before Clara could answer.

Clara sighed heavily. She had hoped to take Scallop.

"Oh, okay," said Clara. "I suppose it's better than not going at all."

CHAPTER 5

Pilwinkle

Lucas ordered a carriage and driver from the royal stables. Soon the children and Ruskin and Percy were off to the Stone Forest. Lucas and Clara played I Spy along the way. Bella rebraided her long blond hair. Clara glanced out the window from time to time to check their progress. Suddenly she leaned forward.

"I see it!" she exclaimed. "The

Stone Forest is on the other side of that river!"

The early afternoon sun shone on a thick forest of stone pillars and arches that towered over the landscape.

"Wow!" exclaimed Lucas. "They

look like the drippy sand castles we make at Mermaid's Cove."

"Only life-size!" added Clara.

The carriage rumbled over the uneven ground. Bella stared at the spires uncertainly.

"I'm not sure if my father would approve of this place," she said. "Are there wild animals?"

"Not that I know of," Clara said. "But you never know."

Bella's eyes grew wide.

"There are *no* wild animals," Lucas assured Bella. "But there doesn't seem to be anyone around either."

The carriage stopped a short way from the towering pillars and arches.

"Look again!" Clara said excitedly.

The children looked carefully at the stone structures. Little faces peeked from the chinks and cracks in the stone.

"Gnomes!" Lucas cried.

Clara smiled and waved at the gnomes. Some of them waved back.

The children hopped out of the carriage.

Clara rushed toward the stone towers. "Hello!" she called.

One by one the gnomes climbed out of their hideouts. The men had lovely long beards, rosy cheeks, and pudgy noses; some of them wore pointed colorful stocking caps. The women and girls wore dresses and had their hair in braids. The boys

wore overalls. The children all wore
red hats with pom-poms on top.

Lucas and Ruskin ran to catch up
to Clara. And Bella stepped daintily
over the pebbly ground in her satin
shoes. She lagged behind, holding
Percy in her arms.

"Wait for me!" she cried.

But Clara was already on to introductions.

"This is Prince Lucas of Wrenly," she said to the gnomes who had gathered to greet them. "And this is his scarlet dragon, Ruskin."

The gnomes smiled and bowed. Clara noticed that the tallest gnome only came up to her chest.

Then Clara pointed to Bella. "That's Princess Bella, and her dog, Percy," she said. "And I'm Clara, a friend of the royal family."

"We're honored to welcome you," said an elder gnome, who leaned on a pickax that was almost the same size as he was. "My name is Pilwinkle."

CHAPTER 6

Tinker's Tower

Bella caught up to the rest of the group and teetered on the uneven ground. Pilwinkle reached out and steadied the princess. But when Bella saw his dirty hands and grimy nails, she shrank back in disgust.

"Ew! Don't you dare touch me!" she cried. "I'm going back to the carriage!"

Then Bella picked up the folds

of her gown and walked carefully toward the carriage. *How embarrassing!* thought Clara. She was glad Lucas didn't try to stop the princess. And the gnomes simply acted as if nothing had happened.

"What can we do for you?" asked
Pilwinkle.

This time Lucas spoke up. "Clara
has come to learn about the Stone
Forest for a school project," he said.
"The princess and I are along for the
adventure—or at least, I am."

"We'd love to show you around," Pilwinkle said. "We only have one rule in the Stone Forest."

"What is it?" asked Clara.

"No one may enter the underground city without a guide," said Pilwinkle. "It's much too easy to get lost."

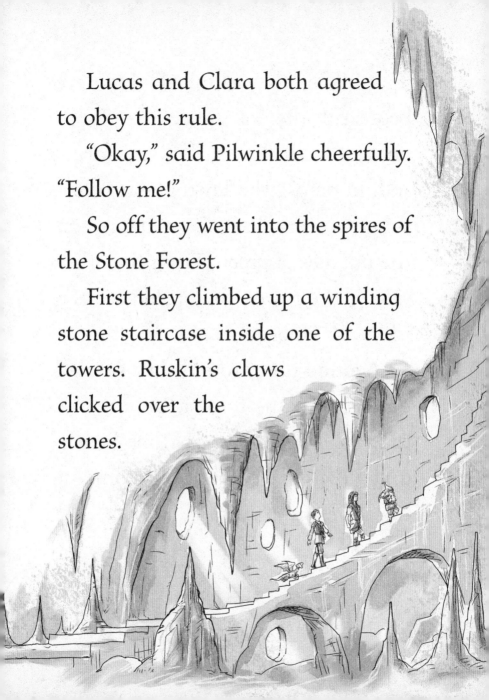

Lucas and Clara both agreed
to obey this rule.

"Okay," said Pilwinkle cheerfully.
"Follow me!"

So off they went into the spires of
the Stone Forest.

First they climbed up a winding
stone staircase inside one of the
towers. Ruskin's claws
clicked over the
stones.

The higher they climbed, the more beautiful the view became. From one side of the tower, they saw farms rolling across the land like a colorful patchwork quilt. Cows grazed on the patches of green. From the other side of the tower, they could see the island of Hobsgrove.

Around and around they swirled until they came to a sitting area at the top. They sat on a stone bench, and Pilwinkle pointed out some of the towers and arches.

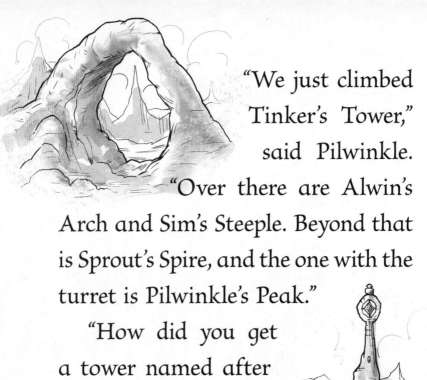

"We just climbed
Tinker's Tower,"
said Pilwinkle.
"Over there are Alwin's
Arch and Sim's Steeple. Beyond that
is Sprout's Spire, and the one with the
turret is Pilwinkle's Peak."

"How did you get
a tower named after
you?" asked Lucas.

"Well, I guess you
have to do something

to help the community," Pilwinkle said.

"And what have you done to receive such a great honor?" Lucas asked.

Pilwinkle chuckled. "I've been the chief gnome for more than fifty years," he said. "When you've been in charge that long, you get a tower named after you. It reminds me to be my best."

CHAPTER 7

Damsel in Distress

Ruskin scampered to the edge of the tower and squawked.

"Excuse me, Pilwinkle," Lucas said. Then he rushed to his dragon's side. "What is it, Ruskin?"

Clara and Pilwinkle joined them. They heard barking down below.

Yip! Yap! Yip! Yap!

"It sounds like Percy!" said Lucas. They all carefully peeked over

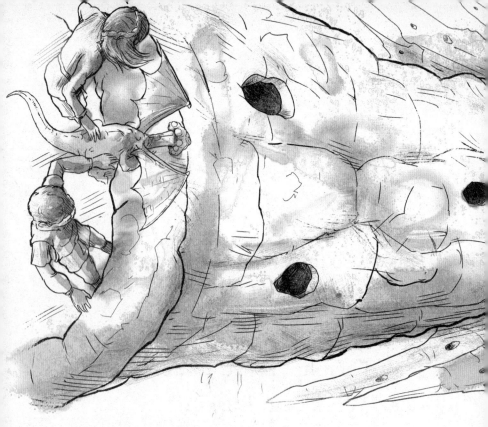

the edge of the tower.

"That's because it *is* Percy!" Clara
cried.

They watched as Percy chased
a squirrel and Bella stumbled after

them. She tripped over her gown with every step.

"Percy, come back here!" Bella shouted.

But Percy bounded farther away.

The squirrel jumped into a tunnel, and Percy scampered in after it.

"No!" shrieked Bella. She cupped her hand over her mouth.

She tottered toward the entrance to the tunnel.

"Help!" she cried. "Someone help me save Percy!"

"Uh-oh," Pilwinkle said. "The princess and her dog could get lost. We need to find them right away." Pilwinkle raced toward the stairs. "Right behind you!" Lucas cried.

Ruskin scampered after Lucas.

Oh no! thought Clara as she ran after them. *I hope nothing bad happens to Bella and Percy!*

Pilwinkle whistled at the bottom of the stone stairs. "Lumbiddle! Wayrich! Dalfoodle!" he shouted to his nearby fellow gnomes. "We need your help! The princess and her little white dog have entered the underground without a guide."

The three gnomes rushed toward Pilwinkle.

"Lumbiddle, grab the torches!" Pilwinkle directed.

He quickly got several torches from a wooden box and passed them around.

"This way!" Pilwinkle shouted.

CHAPTER 8

Underground

Everyone followed Pilwinkle into the tunnel. Lumbiddle lit the torches one by one as they entered. The tunnel opened into a wide chamber and a busy marketplace. Gnomes sat on stone benches and at tables in front of the market. Four tunnels went off in different directions from the main chamber.

Suddenly, Bella came running

toward them. "I can't find Percy!" she cried.

"Don't worry," said Lucas, putting his arm around her. "We'll find him."

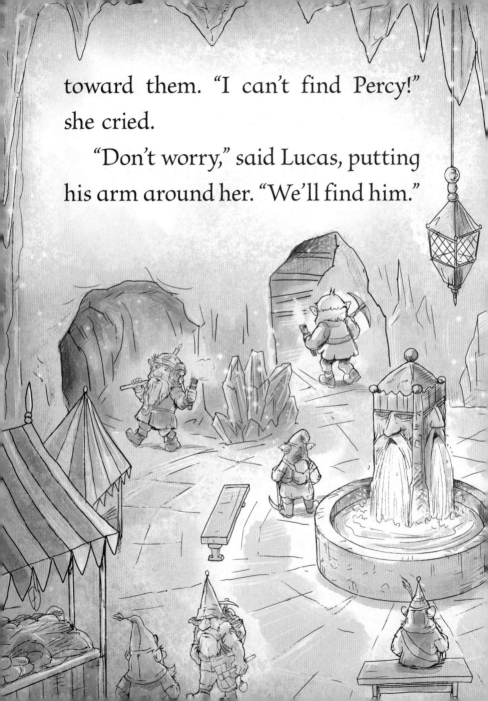

"Let's split up," Pilwinkle said. "Children and Ruskin, come with me. Everyone else take a separate tunnel. We'll meet back here."

Pilwinkle lead the way down a
stone staircase.

"Percy!" they called. "Here, Percy!
Come on, boy!"

The tunnel opened into a wide
cavern. Jagged crystals covered the

walls and ceiling like thousands of ice swords and icicles. The crystals shimmered in the torchlight.

They walked along a stone path in the middle of the cavern.

"It looks like a magical crystal

palace!" exclaimed Clara.

Lucas and Bella turned around in a circle. The crystals swirled in a rainbow of color. Pilwinkle stayed focused.

"Percy!" he called. "Come on, little puppy!"

Everyone listened for Percy's bark, but all they heard was a waterfall up ahead. Bella sniffled and wiped her eyes with a handkerchief.

The children followed Pilwinkle across a long, beautiful bridge. The

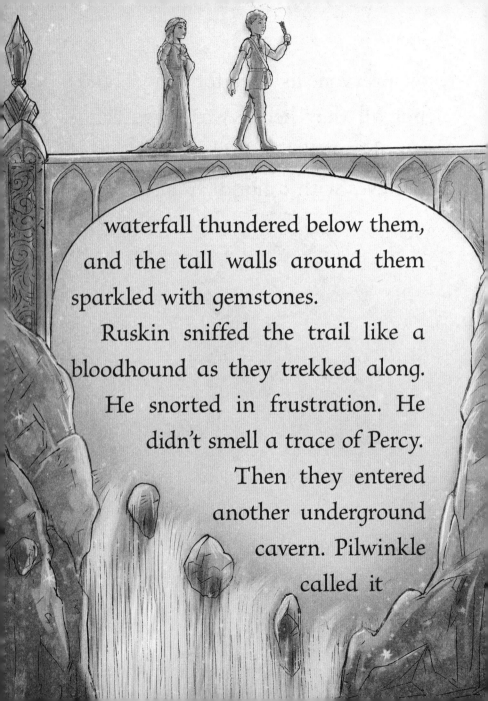

waterfall thundered below them, and the tall walls around them sparkled with gemstones.

Ruskin sniffed the trail like a bloodhound as they trekked along. He snorted in frustration. He didn't smell a trace of Percy. Then they entered another underground cavern. Pilwinkle called it the Den of Diamonds. Thousands of diamonds dotted the sides and the top of the cavern, twinkling like stars at night. The children waved their torches in search of Percy. The light made the diamonds shine more brightly. Clara wanted to lie down and gaze at the starry gems, but they had no time to lose.

"Percy!" she called. "Percy, where are you?"

Bella stared into the pool of water and began to cry. "What if my dog is lost forever?"

Pilwinkle hurried over to Bella and put his arm around her. "Come now, Princess," he said gently. "You must be strong for Percy. He needs you to find him."

Bella leaned on Pilwinkle. Her feet hurt from running in her good shoes, and her head hurt from crying. She no longer cared about his grubby hands and nails. Instead, she felt comforted by his kind words.

Pilwinkle led Bella and the other

children down another tunnel. They passed a gnome village with homes and stores—all lighted by torchlight and lanterns. They called for Percy all along the way. But still there was no answer. They began to circle back to the main chamber.

Ruskin sniffed the ground more eagerly as they went. Then he squawked loudly.

"What is it, boy?" cried Lucas. "Do you smell Percy?"

Ruskin kept sniffing. Pilwinkle, Clara, and the princess joined him. Pilwinkle examined the ground.

"Paw prints!" he cried.

"I don't see anything," said Bella, searching the ground.

"Me neither," agreed Lucas and Clara together.

"Gnomes have great eyesight," said Pilwinkle. "Come on!"

The children and Ruskin followed Pilwinkle. Then the passage-
way stopped abruptly.

"Oh no!" wailed Bella. "A dead
end!"

CHAPTER 9

Friends

But Ruskin continued to sniff the wall in front of him. Then he stood on his hind legs and whined. Tucked on a ledge sat Percy, shaking from head to tail.

Pilwinkle carefully scooped Percy into his arms and handed him to Bella.

"Percy, you're filthy!" she scolded as she rocked her dog like a baby.

"But I'm so glad to see you!"

Then Bella, with her own face smudged with dirt and tears, looked down at Pilwinkle. "I'm sorry I was mean to you," she said softly.

The gnome smiled and patted Bella on the back.

"I now realize that every member of the kingdom is as important as a royal," said Bella.

"I'm glad I could help," he said.

"You helped me too!" Clara said. "You've shown me one of the most beautiful lands in Wrenly."

"And there's still so much to see," Pilwinkle said.

"There is?" questioned Clara.

Pilwinkle grinned. "You have yet to see the River of Rubies," he said, stroking his beard. "There's also the Emerald Oasis and the Fountain of Sapphires. We even have the Pearly Gates, a cavern filled with freshwater pearls."

After climbing out of the caverns, Clara crouched by a small stone stump. She could hardly take it all in. She wrote every detail

on one of her animal hides. She listed the things she had seen and the things she would see another time. Then she sat down and finished her sketches of the Stone Forest.

"I'll bet you'll get the highest mark in your class," Bella said, watching over Clara's shoulder.

101

Clara stopped sketching and looked at Bella.

"You know what?" said Clara, smiling. "I think I'm beginning to like you."

Bella blushed. "Thanks," she said. "You're not so bad either."

Lucas looked at the girls and

smiled. Then Ruskin squawked in approval.

The girls giggled.

Pilwinkle looked toward the hills. "You should all get going. The sun is setting, and I'm sure your parents will want you home before dark."

Bella curtsied to Pilwinkle. "Thank you again," said the princess. "You are a really great friend."

"Why, thank *you*, Bella," said Pilwinkle with a bow. "You know, good friends are more precious than all the gemstones here."

The children said good-bye to Pilwinkle and walked toward the carriage. Bella carried Percy, and

Ruskin scampered behind. They sat down in the carriage and looked at one another.

"Oh no," Lucas said.

"What?" asked Bella.

"Look at us!" said Lucas. "We're a mess!"

Smudges of dirt covered their faces and good clothes.

"It's just a little dirt!" said Bella.

Then they all burst out laughing.

CHAPTER 10

A Good Report

Clara stood in front of her class. She was the last one to give her geography report.

"Sometimes the most beautiful place on earth is right under your nose," she began. "And I found that place. It's a place I had passed many times—and maybe you have too—but I had never been inside."

Clara walked over to the map of

Wrenly. "I visited the Stone Forest," she continued. "It is located to the southeast of Mermaid's Cove and overlooks Hobsgrove on one side. This enchanted city was built entirely by gnomes over hundreds of years."

Clara held up an animal hide to show her sketches of the Stone Forest.

"Not only are the arches and towers beautiful, but you can also climb up winding stairs inside and outside the structures. The views of Wrenly are amazing! Underneath the spires is a stunning underground world. There is more treasure in these tunnels than in all the fairy tales ever written."

Then Clara told the story of Princess Bella and her missing dog. She described Pilwinkle, the other gnomes, and the caverns of crystals and jewels. She showed her class-mates the route they had taken through the tunnels and described what they had seen.

"An entire world exists beneath the Stone Forest," said Clara. "There are homes, stores, roads, bridges, and tumbling waterfalls. But the best part about the Stone Forest was the new friends I made."

Clara pulled out two more animal hides. One had a sketch of Pilwinkle, and the other one had a sketch of Princess Bella.

"We will be friends forever," said Clara, ending her report.

Mistress Carson and the children clapped for Clara. Clara handed her animal hides to her teacher. Then the children ran outside for lunch and recess.

Mistress Carson stayed behind and pulled out a needle and thread. She began to sew the children's animal hides together.

A few days later, Mistress Carson finished the tapestry. When sewn together, the pieces of hide formed

a map of the kingdom. She hung
it in the classroom for everyone to
admire.

Hear ye! Hear ye!
Presenting the next book from
The Kingdom of Wrenly!
Here's a sneak peek!

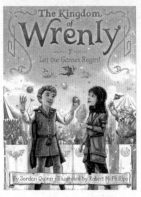

A boy walked toward them. He had a picture of a lion on his jacket—the symbol of the Knight of Thornwood. The squire bowed before the prince.

"Good morning, Your Highness," he said. "My name is Gilbert. I'm Sir Hugh's squire."

"Pleased to meet you, Gilbert," said Lucas. "You must be very talented to serve Sir Hugh!"

Excerpt from *Let the Games Begin!*

"Yes, what a great honor!" Clara added.

Gilbert paid no attention to Clara. He kept his eyes on Lucas. "Sir Hugh is a great teacher. Would you like me to introduce you?"

"Would I ever!" cried Lucas. "Sir Hugh is my all-time favorite hero."

"Mine too!" agreed Gilbert.

"Ahem," said Clara, trying to be part of the conversation. "Someday I hope to become a knight too!"

This got Gilbert's attention. He looked at her and laughed. Even Lucas looked surprised.

Excerpt from *Let the Games Begin!*

"Girls can't be knights!" declared Gilbert.

"And why not?" questioned Clara, folding her arms.

"Because all knights are *boys!*" argued Gilbert.

"That doesn't mean a girl can't be one!" Clara shot back.

"A *girl* knight?" said Gilbert. "Are you kidding?"

"No!" Clara said firmly. "I can be whatever I want—so long as I work hard enough for it."

Gilbert raised his arms in the air. "Who *is* this girl?" he cried.

Excerpt from *Let the Games Begin!*